Disco Divas

Follow the Glitter Girls' latest adventures!
Collect the other fantastic books in the series:

Caroline Plaisted

Disco Divas

■SCHOLASTIC

★ ♥ ★ ♥ ★ ♥ ★

Scholastic Children's Books,
Commonwealth House, 1-19 New Oxford Street,
London WC1A 1NU, UK
a division of Scholastic Ltd

London ~ New York ~ Toronto ~ Sydney ~ Auckland
Mexico City ~ New Delhi ~ Hong Kong

Published by Scholastic Ltd, 2001

Copyright © Caroline Plaisted, 2001

ISBN 0 439 99403 9

Typeset by Falcon Oast Graphic Art Ltd.
Printed and bound in Great Britain by Cox & Wyman Ltd, Reading, Berks.

2 4 6 8 10 9 7 5 3 1

★ ♥ ★ ♥ ★ ♥ ★

Chapter 1

Hannah and Meg were having a great time plaiting and braiding each other's hair. They were waiting in Meg's bedroom for their friends Charly, Zoe and Flo to come and join them.

"Hey, that's great!" said Hannah, admiring the pink and purple beads that Meg had woven into her long red hair.

"We're just so lucky that we learnt all this hair stuff for the Magical Makeovers at the school fête, aren't we?" said Meg.

Meg and Hannah were so busy chatting away as they played with their hair that they didn't hear the first knock on Meg's bedroom door. The Glitter Girls had a special "RAT tat tat" knock that they always used before they entered each other's bedrooms. But Meg and Hannah did hear the second, much louder tapping, and the girls stopped nattering and looked towards the door.

"Who's there?" Meg asked.

"GG!" came the whispered reply.

Immediately, Meg rushed over to the door, knowing that one of the other Glitter Girls had arrived. "GG" was the Glitter Girls' secret password. When she opened the door, Flo was standing there, holding a huge jug of juice in one hand and some glasses in the other.

"Hi Flo!" said Meg and Hannah together.

"Hey, you two!" Flo replied, putting the jug and glasses down carefully on the chest of drawers.

It was Friday afternoon – the start of the weekend! When the Glitter Girls met up it was usually very soon after they had got home from school. But on Fridays it was different because Zoe and Charly went off to their riding lesson straight from school. So the Glitter Girls met up later, usually after five o'clock, so that they all had time to change out of their school uniform.

When they weren't at school, the Glitter Girls loved to wear cool clothes that were pink or purple and lots of sparkly and glittery accessories. It was one of the reasons they were known as the Glitter Girls!

"Your mum thought we might need a drink," said Flo. "Great!" said Meg, pouncing on the juice and starting to pour it out for her friends. She had only just handed out the glasses when there was another knock on the door.

"Who is it?" Meg asked again.

"GG!" came the reply, and Meg quickly opened the door to let both Zoe and Charly in.

Now the Glitter Girls meeting could really begin!

Chapter 2

Charly and Zoe bundled into Meg's bedroom, each carrying a plate full of sandwiches that Meg's mum had given them. None of them wasted any time before tucking in!

Meg was the most organized of the Glitter Girls. Her room was always neat and tidy. Her mum never had to nag her to sort it out! She played the cello and in her room she kept the most scrumptious translucent pink music stand. None of the other Glitter Girls played an instrument (apart from the recorder, like everyone else at school), but all of them wanted to have the music stand!

"Great hair!" Zoe said, looking at Meg and Hannah.

Meg had long, wavy blonde hair and Hannah had created a mass of tiny plaits all around her head too. She'd even woven in some pretty ribbons amongst the strands of hair.

"It's wicked, isn't it?" said Meg, smiling. "Hannah did it."

"Wow, Hannah!" said Charly. "You haven't forgotten the Magical Makeovers stuff then! Will you do mine again soon?"

Hannah was pretty pleased with it herself and she smiled with satisfaction. "Course," she said. "So, how was your riding lesson?"

"Cool!" Charly replied. "We did some little jumps today, didn't we?"

"Yes – it was really good!" Zoe replied. "And we heard all about some new donkeys that have arrived at the Donkey Sanctuary, too!"

The Donkey Sanctuary was one of the Glitter Girls' favourite places to visit and they went there at least once every holiday. They'd first found out about the Donkey Sanctuary through Charly and

Zoe's trips to the riding stables. One of the ladies who ran the stables had told them about the Sanctuary because she had adopted a donkey that was living there. The Sanctuary looked after donkeys that had no one else to care for them, or donkeys that were very old and needed somewhere peaceful to spend their days grazing.

The first time the Glitter Girls had visited the Sanctuary they had fallen completely in love with all the donkeys that lived there.

As soon as the Donkey Sanctuary was mentioned, the other Glitter Girls stopped their munching and bombarded Charly and Zoe with questions.

"What new donkeys?" Flo asked.

"Yes – when did they arrive there?" Meg wanted to know.

"Well," said Charly, pushing her pink glasses back up her nose. "The donkeys have come from the seaside. They used to spend almost every day working on the beach."

"Doing what?" Meg wanted to know.

"They used to take children for rides up and down the beach," Zoe said.

"Ohhh!" Hannah said. She thought back to last year when she had gone on holiday with her mum, dad and brother to Spain. She and Joe had gone the whole length of the beach riding on donkeys. They even had a photograph of them doing it in the downstairs loo at home!

"So, what are their names?" Flo asked.

"That's the thing – no one knows!" Charly said. "It's really sad. . ."

"What do you mean, no one knows?" Hannah looked up indignantly. "Surely the person who looked after them at the beach must know their names!"

"Yes!" said Flo, twiddling her hair and sucking her thumb. Flo still sucked her thumb, but none of the Glitter Girls mentioned it. It was just another of the things that made her special!

"But that's what's so sad!" Zoe said. "The man

who owned the donkeys died, and no one else can remember what he called them."

"Oh no!" said Hannah, who hated hearing sad stories. "But didn't he have any family? Surely *they* know what the donkeys are called?"

"I don't think he did," Charly said. "After the man died, no one knew what to do with the donkeys. So the local authority down at the beach asked the Donkey Sanctuary if they'd take them."

"And that's how they came to be there," said Zoe.

"Well, we've got to go and see them, haven't we?" Meg begged her friends.

"Yes, we have!" Hannah agreed.

"It's Saturday tomorrow," said Flo. "Why don't we go then?"

"Good idea!" Charly looked at her friends, smiling at the thought of a trip to one of their favourite places.

"Hold on," said Meg, who was always so

practical and organized. "How are we going to get there?"

"That's a point," Hannah mumbled, looking disappointed.

"I'm sure one of our mums or dads will take us," suggested Charly.

"I've got an idea," said Meg, thoughtfully. "I'm spending the day with my dad to-morrow. . ." Meg and her brother and sister lived with their mum but they didn't live with their dad, ". . . he's taking me out on my own for the day while Jack and Sue go somewhere with Mum. I'll phone him tonight and ask him if he'll take us to the Donkey Sanctuary!"

"Good one!" said Charly.

"Brilliant idea!" agreed Flo.

The Glitter Girls looked around at each other. They were all smiling at the thought of visiting the new arrivals at the Sanctuary. All at once, they all put their hands in the air and said, victoriously, "GO GLITTER!"

Chapter 3

It was Saturday morning and Meg had success-fully persuaded her dad to take the Glitter Girls to see the donkeys.

"Excuse me," Zoe said to the lady behind the reception desk, "can you tell me which stable the new donkeys are in?"

The lady looked up, and the girls noticed that she was wearing a really great T-shirt with a pic-ture of a donkey's head on the front.

"Oh, they've been let out into a paddock on their own," the lady replied, smiling back at her. "My goodness, they've only been here a few days – trust you girls to know they are here!" She knew the Glitter Girls from their regular visits during the holidays. "Turn right out of here and head down to the bottom," she said, and she pointed to a paddock over at the far side of the Sanctuary.

"Thanks!" the Glitter Girls all said at once, and they set off, following the directions. It was Zoe who caught sight of them first and instinctively she started to run towards the two donkeys, who had their heads down, grazing. The others, except for Meg's dad, kept up with her and, as they got closer, the girls could see that one of the donkeys was slightly bigger and fluffier than the other.

"Oh look! Aren't they gorgeous?" said Charly, when they reached the paddock.

The smaller donkey raised its head and looked curiously at the girls, as if it was wondering who they were.

"Look!" said Flo. "This one's got a sort of pink stripe running down its nose!"

"They are so cute!" Charly sighed.

"Hey! There's a notice about them here," Hannah went over to the paddock gate, where a white sign had been pinned up. "It says that they're two females. They came from the seaside, where they lived for ten years giving rides to children up and down the beach. Then it says the bit about not knowing their names, like Charly and Zoe said," she called back over her shoulder to the others.

Meg joined Hannah at the gate. "Let's see." She stopped next to Hannah and read the notice herself. "Hey – it's asking people to think of names for the donkeys! Aren't they cute!"

"They certainly are," said Flo.

"I hope they come over to see us," said Charly, leaning over the fence.

By the time Meg's dad had managed to catch up with the Glitter Girls, they were all lined up on the bottom rung of the paddock fence, trying to catch the donkeys' attention.

"You girls move fast, don't you?" said Mr

Morgan, panting. He leant on the fence and tried to catch his breath.

"Aren't they cute, Dad?" Meg asked him.

"They certainly seem like fine donkeys," he said, as he too began to read the sign.

After a few minutes, the two donkeys stopped their eating and the bigger donkey went over to join her companion. They seemed to be nuzzling each other's heads. It looked as if they were talking to each other. Suddenly, both the donkeys looked up and gazed at the Glitter Girls.

"Hello, you two!" Flo whispered softly to them.

The donkeys didn't move at first. Then the bigger one seemed to be gently nudging the other donkey forward with her nose.

"Hey, look!" said Meg. "Did you see that?"

"Come and say hello to us!" Zoe pleaded softly, desperate to be able to stroke their necks.

Quietly, Charly jumped down from the fence

and grabbed a handful of grass in her hand. Then she climbed back up on to the fence and held out the grass to the two donkeys.

"Here you go," she said gently. "Lovely fresh grass for you."

The sight of the delicious grass made the already curious donkeys want to wander closer. Very slowly, the nameless pair trotted over towards the Glitter Girls.

"They're coming to see us!" Meg whispered.

The donkeys headed straight to Charly's hand and, after a few nervous seconds, the bigger one took the grass from her and munched away happily. Her smaller companion looked really cross!

"Here, cutey," Flo jumped down, grabbed a handful of grass and offered it to the little donkey. The donkey took it from her and looked happier again.

"They are soooo sweet!" said Hannah.

"The big one's got such a soft and fluffy

coat," Zoe said. "I wonder if she'll let me stroke her."

The other Glitter Girls watched as their friend gently rubbed her hand down the donkey's neck. She certainly didn't mind – in fact the donkey looked like she was enjoying it, and she nuzzled Zoe back.

"Hello Fluffball," Zoe said to her.

"She really is fluffy, isn't she?" Meg leant over the fence and she too gently stroked the donkey. The more attention the donkey got, the more she seemed to enjoy it! And the more cross the other donkey seemed to get!

After a few minutes, the little donkey walked over to her four-legged friend and gently, but firmly, bumped her neck with her head. When that didn't stop the fluffy donkey from making friends with Zoe and Meg, the little donkey turned round to Charly and softly biffed her head at Charly's hand.

"She wants you to stroke her!" Flo gasped.

"I think she does," Charly giggled, and then she tickled the dear little donkey behind the ears with both of her hands.

"Isn't her nose cute?" Hannah said, looking at the very clear pink blaze that ran along the length of the little donkey's nose.

"It's much paler than the rest of her, isn't it?" said Charly.

"It's kind of a pinky colour," Flo leant over to the donkey and ran her hand down the length of it.

"Well, you girls certainly seem to have made friends with the new donkeys," Meg's dad said. "Listen, why don't I go back to the stable block and see if I can buy some carrots for you to feed them?"

"Yesss!" they all cried.

Chapter 4

The donkeys loved carrots and the Glitter Girls spent a happy time feeding and stroking them. It was just starting to rain when Tim, one of the people that ran the Donkey Sanctuary, came over to the paddock. Tim was the eldest brother of one of the boys in year six at the Glitter Girls' school. He was really friendly and had been working at the Sanctuary ever since he'd left secondary school.

"Hello again," he said, putting down a big bucket of water. "I see you've been making friends with our newcomers. They're friendly things, aren't they?" He carried on talking to the Glitter Girls as he greeted the two donkeys and then filled their trough with water from his bucket.

"Yes," said Zoe. "Do you really not have names for them?"

"Afraid we haven't at the moment. Did you see the board we put up asking people to suggest names for them?"

"Yes!" Meg said. "We're really good at things like that!"

"Yes," Flo agreed. "We'll definitely help with some name ideas."

"We could certainly do with your help! And you could tell all your friends at school to come and see them as well. We need to raise some extra money to help feed these two and care for them."

"Course we'll tell them!" Charly exclaimed. "I'm sure everyone at school will come and see them!"

"Do you need to raise much money for them then?" Hannah asked.

Tim put down the bucket and wiped his forehead with his sleeve. "Afraid so," he said.

"We run this place on a shoestring you see. Being a charity, every penny is accounted for. We've got the space for them, but if we don't raise the extra cash to feed these new girls here, then we may have to send them to another sanctuary, three hundred kilometres away."

"But that's awful!" said Meg.

"Yes, dreadful!" agreed Charly.

"We'll do anything to help. They're so gorgeous," said Zoe, who was still stroking the fluffy donkey.

By now, the rain was beginning to fall quite heavily.

"Come on, girls," said Meg's dad. "Why don't we all go and have some lunch and then you can come back and have another look at the donkeys afterwards."

"See you girls later then," said Tim, giving them a wave.

"Yes, see you later," Charly waved back.

The Glitter Girls headed over to the little café that was on the other side of the stable block.

"See you later, donkeys!" they all called to their new friends.

Over lunch, the Glitter Girls chatted away with Meg's dad about how cute the donkeys were and how they wanted to help raise money to keep them at the Sanctuary.

"So what would you call them?" Meg's dad asked them.

"Well, they need special names, don't they?" Zoe said.

"Yes – something unusual," Flo said, popping her thumb out of her mouth as she said it.

"Why don't we think of something that reminds them of the time they spent at the seaside?" Charly suggested.

"Good idea!" said Hannah. "How about Punch and Judy!"

"That's a good idea," Meg's dad said, sounding impressed.

"Hang on," said Zoe, "there's already a donkey called Judy here, isn't there? You remember the one that's been here for about two years? She came from that farmer who retired."

"Oh yes," said Hannah, disappointed that her good idea wasn't such a good one after all.

"There must be some other seaside names," Meg's dad said.

"Yes. . ." Meg was thinking out loud. "Like . . . Pebbles?"

"Pebbles is cool, isn't it?" Flo agreed, looking at her other friends for their approval.

"It's not bad," said Charly, "but it sounds like a name for an animal with spots! How about Sandy? Or Ocean?"

"They're OK names – but I'm not convinced they're quite right for them," said Hannah. "I mean, it seems so wrong to give that cute little one a name like Ocean when she's got that pinky face."

"That's it!" Zoe almost shouted with excitement.

"What's it?" Hannah asked.

"She's got a pinky face!" said Zoe.

"What?" asked Flo. "You want to call her Pinky Face?"

"No, you twit! Pink!" said Zoe impatiently.

"Brilliant!" said Meg. "Pink is perfect for her!"

"Yes, let's tell Tim!" said Charly.

"But what about the other one?" asked Meg's dad. "She needs a name too."

"She's all fluffy and cute," said Flo.

"Really fluffy," agreed Zoe.

"Got it!" said Meg triumphantly. "Fluffy!"

"That's her!" Hannah said. "We'll find Tim before we leave and see what he thinks of our suggestions!"

As they finished their lunch, the girls started

thinking of ideas to help raise funds for the two donkeys.

"We could get sponsored for something," Meg suggested.

"And we could come and help out here during the holidays," said Flo.

"We've got to help, haven't we?" Hannah asked her friends. They all agreed with her.

After lunch, the Glitter Girls took Meg's dad on a tour of the Donkey Sanctuary. He'd never been there before so they introduced him to all of their donkey friends that they'd got to know during their visits.

Their tour finished at the paddock where they'd begun. This time, the two donkeys didn't hesitate to come over and greet the Glitter Girls – the donkeys knew the girls obviously already were their friends. As the Glitter Girls were saying their goodbyes and promising to come back soon, Tim arrived to take the donkeys back to their stable.

"Enjoy your lunch, you lot?" he asked.

"Yes thanks," the Glitter Girls all said at once.

"And we've got some ideas for names too!" said Zoe.

"Oh really, what are they?" asked Tim.

"Pink and Fluffy!" said Flo.

"Pink for her," Hannah pointed to the smaller donkey, "because of her pink face."

"And Fluffy for her," said Zoe, "because of her fluffy coat!"

"Well, they sound quite good," said Tim. "Tell you what, why don't I mention those names to the rest of the staff and see what they think?"

"Yes please!" said Meg.

"When will we know if you've chosen them?" Flo asked.

"I expect we'll know quite soon. Hey, if you girls are serious about getting your friends to help raise money for the donkeys, why don't you come back next week and we'll let you in for half price. If you bring some carrots to feed the donkeys with, of course!"

"Course we're serious!" said Meg. "We've already been talking about what we can do to help."

"Go Glitter!" the girls cried, raising their arms in the air.

It looked like this was the beginning of another adventure for the Glitters!

Chapter 5

The Glitter Girls were buzzing with excitement as they went home in Meg's dad's car.

"Do you think they *will* call them Pink and Fluffy?" Flo asked no one in particular.

"Wouldn't it be great if they did?" Hannah said.

"We've got to tell everyone at school about them, haven't we?" said Charly. "So that we can get people to raise some money for them."

"Definitely!" said Zoe.

"We could do some makeovers again!" suggested Flo.

"We could," agreed Meg, "but we should really do something different, don't you think?"

"We could get people to pay to suggest

names for the donkeys!" Hannah exclaimed.

"Hmm . . ." Zoe thought for a minute. "But I'm not sure if that will raise very much, will it?"

"No. . ." Hannah sighed. What Zoe said was true, after all.

"We need a meeting!" Meg said firmly.

"That's my Meg!" her dad said, smiling at his youngest daughter. "Organizing everyone as always."

The Glitter Girls laughed kindly at their friend. They could always rely on Meg to help them get things sorted.

Just then, Meg's dad pulled up outside Meg's house. Her mum and her brother and sister must have already got back because her mum's car was parked outside.

"Thanks for taking us, Dad," Meg said, as she waved him goodbye.

"Yes, thanks Mr Morgan," the others said, all waving as well.

"Come on – let's see what my mum's got us

for tea!" Meg shouted, as they all bundled into her house.

★ ♥ ★ ♥ ★ ♥ ★

Over a delicious tea, the Glitter Girls told the rest of Meg's family all about their day at the Donkey Sanctuary.

"They sound really sweet," said Mrs Morgan, taking a sip of her tea.

"Yes," Hannah sighed. The more she thought about Pink and Fluffy (how she hoped that they would end up being called that!), the more she missed them already.

"Sounds like you need to start saving up your pocket money to help with the fund for looking after them," said Jack, Meg's brother.

"We'll need more than our pocket money to help the donkeys though," Flo said thoughtfully.

"I know!" Zoe stood up quickly, almost knocking over her glass of juice in her excitement. "We could get everyone at school to help out with something!"

"Yes!" Charly was as excited as Zoe at the thought. "But what?"

"I'm sure you'll think of something," said Jack. "Just as long as it doesn't need another radio programme!" he teased. Jack had helped out the Glitter Girls when they had volunteered at the local hospital radio station. The Glitter Girls had broadcast a radio programme called *Glitter FM* and Jack had been there to line up the CDs and help them out with the technical stuff.

"Sounds like you girls need to have one of your meetings," Mrs Morgan suggested. Like all of their mums, she knew that the Glitter Girls liked to get together to talk about their exciting ideas and plan their schemes.

"Let's do it now!" said Meg, grabbing one of her notebooks that was sitting on the worktop in the kitchen. Meg loved making lists of things that had to be done.

"But I can't!" wailed Charly. "My mum wants

me home by five." Charly looked at her watch. It was exactly the same as Flo's: they both had watches that looked like pink bubbles with matching bubbly straps.

"I've got to go soon as well," said Hannah. "Mum and Dad are going out tonight and my gran's coming to look after us."

"Me too," said Flo. "It's my mum's birthday today and me and my sister are helping my dad to make her a special Chinese meal." Flo's dad was half Chinese and a fantastic cook. He often made the Glitter Girls a delicious Chinese meal and they loved it!

"Oh well," Meg was disappointed that they wouldn't be able to get their plans into action straight away. But she could understand why her friends weren't able to stay.

"Tell you what," said Charly, putting her glass down and getting ready to go, "why don't you all come round to my house tomorrow after-noon? We can talk about the donkeys then."

"Good idea!" said Zoe.

"You're on!" Hannah and Flo said at the same time.

"Sounds cool," said Meg.

"Go Glitter!" the girls all said at once.

By two o'clock the next afternoon, the Glitter Girls meeting was in progress. They were all sitting in a circle in Charly's bedroom, surrounded by all of her special animal and television posters.

"We could make some craft things – like the scrunchies we made for the Magical Makeovers stall – and sell them at a craft fair," said Hannah.

Last term, the Glitter Girls had run a makeovers stall at the school fête, painting nails and braiding hair and things. With the help of Charly's and Hannah's mum (who made costumes for a theatre), the Glitter Girls had made some scrunchies. They were a great success and had sold out well before the end of the fête.

"Yes!" said Zoe, excited as usual. "We could make other things too, like friendship bracelets and stuff, and sell them in the playground at breaktime!"

"OK – let's ask Mrs Wadhurst about it," said Meg, writing down all the ideas on a big pink notebook. She was writing with a silver pen that wrote with purple ink! She'd found them both the last time she visited Girl's Dream, one of the Glitter Girls' favourite shops – it sold everything the Glitter Girls could ever want.

"We could get the school football team to have a sponsored match!" suggested Flo. Meg scribbled it down on her pad along with all the other suggestions.

"And we could have a No Uniform Day!" said Hannah, who was always keen on the idea of going to school in something pink and gorgeous instead of her uniform!

"Good idea," said Zoe. "Everyone could donate fifty pence for not wearing uniform!"

By the end of the meeting, she had a long list of fund-raising ideas. They included a sponsored silence, a cake sale, a jumble sale, the football match and the craft ideas.

"They all sound great," said Hannah. "But don't we need something big to get everyone's attention?"

"I know what you mean. . ." Zoe pondered.

"We could ask Mrs Wadhurst to mention it in assembly," Meg suggested. Mrs Wadhurst was the headteacher at the Glitter Girls' school. "Then she could ask if the others can do something special to raise some money."

"Yes – like I could get my gran to pay me to do extra ballet practice between lessons!" Hannah was really keen on ballet. In fact, she wanted to be a ballet dancer one day.

"That'd be cool," agreed Meg. "Shall we ask Mrs Wadhurst, then?"

"Yes," said Zoe. "But I think we still need to come up with a big event that everyone can support."

"Something different. . ." said Charly.

"How about a show?" asked Flo.

"It would take a lot of organizing," said Zoe. "Anyway, there's going to be a show by the local theatre group soon. We don't want to stop people from going to that, do we?"

"No, you're right," Meg put down her pen.

"What about a concert then?" Charly asked. "We could get people to pay to enter."

"Could do. . ." said Flo. "But that'd also be a lot of work!"

"I know. . ." said Hannah, "what about a disco?"

"Yes!" said Charly and Flo excitedly.

"Brilliant!" said Zoe.

"My mum could borrow the lights and stuff from the theatre," said Hannah. "At least, I could ask her if she could!"

"And Jack might help us with the music and things," Meg suggested. "We know he's good at cueing CDs and stuff, don't we?" Meg giggled, thinking about what Jack had said at tea the day before.

"We could sell tickets at school!" Zoe shouted.

"And at riding," added Charly.

"I could sell some at ballet!" said Hannah.

"And I'll see if anyone at my music lesson wants some," said Meg. She played the cello. In fact, she was really good at it.

"I know!" said Flo, looking like she'd had a really, really brilliant idea – which she had! "We could call it a Donkey Disco! Because we're raising money for the donkeys!"

"Just one problem," said Meg, tapping the end of her pen on her lips.

"What's the problem?" asked Zoe.

"Where are we going to have this disco?" Meg asked her friends. "And when?"

"Do you think we could have it at school?"

asked Charly. "In the school hall. It would be perfect!"

"Yes!" agreed Zoe and Hannah.

"Well we'd better ask Mrs Wadhurst on Monday then!" Charly declared, and the others agreed.

"Go Glitter!" all of them screamed at once!

Chapter 6

At school on Monday morning, the Glitter Girls could think of nothing else but Pink and Fluffy.

"What are we going to do if they don't want to call them that?" Flo sighed. "I mean, the names just suit them so well."

"They do, don't they?" said Meg. "Listen, I've asked Miss Stanley if we can go along to see Mrs Wadhurst. She said she'd have a word with her before lessons this morning and then we can perhaps see her at break."

"Oh, well done Meg!" said Hannah.

"Do you think she'll say it's OK?" Charly wondered.

"I hope so!" said Meg. "Then we can get started with all our plans!"

Just then, the bell went. It was time to try to stop thinking about the donkeys and get on with some school work.

★ ♥ ★ ♥ ★ ♥ ★

The Glitter Girls did get to see Mrs Wadhurst that day. They met in her office and Meg told her all about the donkeys and how they needed to raise the money to help to keep them at the Sanctuary.

"Well I'm sure that everyone at school will do what they can to help," Mrs Wadhurst smiled at the Glitter Girls. She knew all about the things they did and how they always tried to help other people and have fun at the same time. "Have you got any ideas for fund-raising then? Knowing you girls, I'm sure you've got lots."

So the Glitter Girls told her about the things they'd thought about so far: the crafts, the cake sale, the football match, the No Uniform day – everything.

"And then we've got this great idea about holding a Donkey Disco!" said Meg triumphantly. "We wondered if we could have a disco here, in the school hall. To raise money for the donkeys."

"We could sell the tickets, you see," said Hannah.

Mrs Wadhurst sat back in her chair and twiddled her pen in her fingers. "Well, you *have* thought about it a lot already, haven't you?"

The Glitter Girls nodded in agreement, hoping that she would say yes to the disco.

"So do you think we can go ahead with everything?" Zoe pleaded.

"Well, I need to do some thinking," Mrs Wadhurst said, "and I need to talk to the other teachers as well. A disco would take a lot of organizing if we were going to do it properly."

The Glitter Girls looked at each other, worried that maybe the disco wouldn't happen after all.

Mrs Wadhurst smiled at the girls again. There was a twinkle in her eye as she said, "But of course, a disco would be great fun for everyone, wouldn't it?"

"Yes!" the Glitter Girls agreed.

"Tell you what, then. Let me have a word with the other teachers," Mrs Wadhurst looked at her watch and then started to usher the girls out of her office. " I think I'll call the Donkey Sanctuary as well. Then I'll get back to you later in the week."

★ ♥ ★ ♥ ★ ♥ ★

The beginning of the week seemed to go so slowly! The girls kept asking Mrs Wadhurst if she'd made up her mind but she just kept telling them that there was a lot to discuss, and that they had to be patient. The Glitter Girls didn't know how long they could wait. At least they had another trip to the Sanctuary to look forward to at the weekend!

But on Wednesday afternoon, Zoe arrived at Charly's house after school with a really glum face.

"Here, take a look at this." Zoe took the local newspaper out of her bag and passed it across the kitchen table, where the girls were having something to eat. She looked cross, and it wasn't like Zoe to be cross.

"What's the matter?" Charly asked.

"See for yourself," Zoe snapped. "It's a disaster!"

"Come on, Zoe," Hannah said, "Charly only asked."

"Hmmphh," Zoe mumbled.

The Glitter Girls couldn't understand it, but none of them could think of anything else to say. They picked up the newspaper and started to read it. The front page had a picture of the two new donkeys at the Donkey Sanctuary.

"Hey, it's them!" Meg exclaimed. "Pink and Fluffy!"

All of them could see the headline that accompanied the picture: DRAMA AT DONKEY SANCTUARY.

"What's happened?" Charly asked.

Flo read the newspaper out loud.

"These two gorgeous donkeys have recently arrived at the Donkey Sanctuary. Saved from an uncertain future after their owner died, it was thought that they would spend the rest of their days happy in the security of the loving family environment for which the Donkey Sanctuary is well-known. But the owners of the Sanctuary announced today that funds are now so short that they only have enough money to feed the two new arrivals for a couple of weeks. An urgent appeal has been launched to raise the much needed cash. The Sanctuary owners said today, 'If we can't raise sufficient money, we are afraid that the donkeys will have to be found yet another home'."

The Glitter Girls sat in total silence for a few

moments. They couldn't believe it. Only a few days ago, they were delighted that the two dear little donkeys were their new friends. Now it seemed possible that they'd have to say good-bye to them.

"We can't let it happen!" Hannah said.

"No way!" Meg agreed.

"We won't let them!" Charly was indignant.

"No we won't!" said Flo.

"Yes, but how are we going to stop them?" Zoe asked. The others looked surprised. It wasn't like Zoe to be so down about things.

"Well we're going to raise some money, aren't we?" said Hannah. "Like we agreed. We've already started making plans!"

"Yes, but how are we going to be able to have all those events we talked about in the next two weeks?" Zoe spluttered.

"Zoe's right," Flo said. "I mean, it'll take us two weeks just to organize one of them."

"And then it'll be too late. . ." Charly said, so

quietly that they could only just hear her.

"So, what are we going to do about it?" Meg said determinedly. She was always the one who got things sorted.

"Well, there's not much we can do, is there?" said Hannah.

"We can't just do *nothing*!" Flo said.

"No, but—"

"We can still try!" Charly interrupted. "I mean, we might not be able to do everything we talked about yesterday, but we can't give up now! Everyone's got to help!"

"She's right!" agreed Meg. "Why can't we try? We could get ourselves sponsored to do something – that wouldn't take much planning."

"We could do a sponsored skip!" suggested Hannah.

"Or a sponsored read!" said Meg.

"Or a sponsored silence!" Zoe said. She was beginning to seem a bit more hopeful about the donkeys' plight.

"Perfect," said Meg. "We can go and speak to Mrs Wadhurst about it tomorrow!"

"Yes, she's bound to do everything she can to help!" said Hannah.

"And we could still have a sale of things, couldn't we?" Flo implored. "I mean, we may not have enough time to make loads of crafts but we could do a kind of bring and buy sale."

"Too right!" said Charly. "Mrs Wadhurst will help with that too, I bet."

"But we won't be able to do the disco, will we?" Zoe was looking defeated again.

"No, probably not," agreed Flo.

None of the others tried to disagree. After all, Zoe was right. It looked like the disco was off before it had even begun. . .

Chapter 7

Charly, Zoe, Hannah, Flo and Meg were still worried when they arrived at school the next morning.

"I spoke to Mum about it last night, after you'd all gone," said Charly. "She says she'll help us if we want her to."

"My dad said he'd help us too," said Flo.

"And my mum," said Hannah.

"Well, I suppose that'll help with the bring and buy sale," Zoe agreed reluctantly.

"And my mum said she could come in to school and help us and Mrs Bugden to do some of the baking," said Charly. Mrs Bugden was the school cook.

"I still think we should try to do the disco,"

Meg said. "It could raise a lot of money. I'm going to ask Mrs Wadhurst about it when we see her at break." Few things stopped the determined Meg!

"What's the point?" said Zoe. "How can we possibly raise enough money in the next two weeks to save Pink and Fluffy?"

"Come on, Zoe," Flo put her arm around her friend. "We'll sort it."

"I hope you're right," Zoe sighed, and followed Flo into their classroom.

After only five minutes in Mrs Wadhurst's office at break, the Glitter Girls were feeling much better. She had also seen the local paper and had spoken to the Donkey Sanctuary about what was going on.

"I've already told them that we're going to do everything we can to help. I think we could easily get everyone organized to do a sponsored silence on Friday, don't you, girls?"

Mrs Wadhurst smiled at them.

"I'll do the sponsorship forms on the computer," Flo said. She loved doing things like that.

"That would be good," said Mrs Wadhurst. "And if Charly's mum could arrange the baking for one day next week with Mrs Bugden that would be marvellous. I'll get Mrs Bugden to phone your mother, Charly."

Mrs Wadhurst's words were making even Zoe look a little happier.

"But what about the bring and buy sale?" Hannah asked. "My mum will help with that if she can."

"That will need a bit more work if we need to have it in the next fortnight," Mrs Wadhurst sat back in her chair and tapped her pen on her desk.

"We could send out a notice about it this week and then hold the sale after school one day next week, couldn't we?" Charly pleaded.

"The same day as the cake sale!" suggested Meg.

"That's an excellent idea, Meg. Once everyone is here, they can just spend their money buying everything!" laughed Mrs Wadhurst.

"My mum could help," said Hannah, eagerly.

"And mine!" said Charly.

"OK, let's try," Mrs Wadhurst agreed.

"And what about No Uniform Day?" Flo wondered. "When could we do that?"

"I thought Friday next week," said Mrs Wadhurst. "The teachers decided that they could come in with uniform on instead of you boys and girls. But only if you pay them to do it!"

"Cool!" said Flo, laughing.

"And what about the disco idea we had?" Meg said. She was determined that they should still organize it – even if they did have only two weeks to do it in!

There was a pause. "It would take a lot of

work, girls," Mrs Wadhurst sighed.

The Glitter Girls sat there in silence. It was going to be hard to raise enough money with just the other events. They knew that the disco would raise a lot of money – money that might be able to keep the donkeys at the Sanctuary.

Mrs Wadhurst could see the sad looks on the girls' faces. "Well, we could try to have the disco at school at the end of next week. The same day as No Uniform day. If everyone bought a ticket, that would raise a lot of money, wouldn't it?"

"I'm pretty sure my brother Jack would help with the music," suggested Meg, knowing that her brother wouldn't be able to resist the fame of being a DJ for the night, even if it was for their disco.

"Who would work the lights and stuff though?" Flo asked.

"Mr Wix is good at that sort of thing." Mrs Wadhurst sounded like she'd made up her mind! "But you girls will have to do all the posters and sell the tickets. And, of course, have a word with Mrs Bugden about the food."

"We'll talk to her about it today!" Charly said.

"My mum will help Mr Wix with sorting out the lights and stuff," said Hannah.

"My dad will too!" By this point, Zoe had been cheered up enough to smile too!

"Well, it looks like the fund-raising for the donkeys had better begin! I'll tell everyone about it at the next assembly. Oh, and I'll have a word with Mrs Southgate about the next football match to see if they can get that sponsored. I think there is a match on Saturday," Mrs Wadhurst said. "You girls had better get off and start getting it organized!"

The Glitter Girls looked at each other, smiles beaming from all their faces.

"Go Glitter!"

Chapter 8

It was *such* a busy fortnight for the Glitter Girls! In-between swimming, ballet, music and riding they spent every spare moment organizing their fund-raising ideas. Mrs Wadhurst called a special assembly the same afternoon that she had seen the girls and the whole school was excited about the idea of helping keep the donkeys at the Sanctuary. Every boy and girl at school agreed to do everything they could do to raise the money. One boy in year five even suggested that everyone should give up a week's pocket money to the donkeys and everyone said that they would!

The Glitter Girls set to work straight away on making things, and designing posters and tickets for the various events that they were holding. Immediately after their meeting with Mrs Wadhurst, Flo organized some sponsorship forms for the Sponsored Silence that was happening on Friday. The girls handed them out at school in the afternoon, and they asked everyone they could think of to sponsor them.

"It's a really good cause," they told people, and showed them the article from the newspaper with the photograph of the two adorable donkeys. "We've just got to help to save them!"

On Thursday afternoon the Glitter Girls met up at Flo's house to get everything ready for the bring and buy sale which was happening the following Monday. The Glitter Girls had no difficulty in remembering how to make hair scrunchies and Hannah's mum found them plenty of scraps of fabric. Flo's sister joined in and she helped them to make some badges that read SAVE THE DONKEYS! She'd done the writing in a kind of glittery ink and they looked really cool.

"Hey, I want one!" Meg said as soon as she saw them.

"Only if you give me twenty pence!" Flo said, holding out her hand for the money.

Within days, everyone at school, including the teachers and Mrs Bugden, was wearing a badge!

Zoe had brought along lots of wooden doorstops that her dad had made.

"They're great!" Meg said. "And I've got these cushions that my gran made. She's always doing patchwork stuff for jumble sales and things and she had all these already sewn."

"Brilliant!" said Hannah. "If everyone at school brings something, we'll do really well."

★ ♥ ★ ♥ ★ ♥ ★

At the end of the week, they held the Sponsored Silence. The Glitter Girls' school had never before been so quiet on a Friday afternoon! For the whole of the last hour of school, absolutely everyone sat in complete silence, determined to raise as much money as they could for the two special donkeys that the Glitter Girls had told them all about.

As the bell went at the end of the afternoon, huge cheers erupted from every classroom!

"Don't forget to bring your sponsorship money when you come in on Monday, boys and girls!" Mrs Wadhurst called out, as they all streamed out of the school gates.

★ ♥ ★ ♥ ★ ♥ ★

On Saturday morning, Flo's dad took the Glitter Girls back to the Donkey Sanctuary as they had promised to visit the two donkeys again.

"Have you decided what you are going to call them?" Flo asked Christine, the lady at the reception.

"We haven't yet," she said. "We thought we'd

wait until we know that they're staying here before we give them names."

"But they've got to stay here," Zoe pleaded. "We're trying really hard to raise money for them."

The Glitter Girls told Christine all about the sponsored silence and the other events they were planning.

"We heard from your headteacher that you've been busy," she said, smiling. "When's this disco of yours then?"

"Next Friday," said Meg. "After school."

"You can come if you buy a ticket!" Charly grinned.

"Do you know, I think some of us might just do that," Christine said.

"Can we go and visit Pink and Fluffy now?" Zoe asked. Like all of the girls, she was desperate to see the two donkeys again.

"Now, don't set your heart on those names," Christine warned. "We don't even know if the donkeys are going to stay here yet, let alone what they are going to be called."

"OK," Zoe replied, looking sad.

"Come on," Hannah said, grabbing Zoe's arm. "Let's go and see our two new friends."

The donkeys were in the same paddock that they'd been in last week. They seemed to recognize the Glitter Girls as they came straight over to see them and were obviously expecting to be given something to eat. Fortunately, Flo's dad had brought lots of carrots with him and the donkeys wasted no time in seeking them out.

"Aren't they gorgeous?" Hannah said to no one in particular.

"I can see why you girls are so keen to save them," Flo's dad replied.

Just then, Tim appeared, carrying a large bale of hay.

"Hello again," he said. "I see you've come back to see the donkeys like you said."

"Yes," said Meg. "And we're going to make sure they're here *every* time we come, too!"

Excitedly, the Glitter Girls told him all about the ideas they had for raising the money to keep the donkeys.

"We've already had the Sponsored Silence," Charly explained. "So we'll know on Monday if we've got off to a good start with our fund-raising."

"It sounds fantastic," said Tim. "I'll look forward to hearing how you get on next weekend. We've already raised five hundred pounds but we need to double that to make sure the donkeys will be all right," he said, picking up the bale of hay that he had put down next to the paddock. "Right, must get on, girls. I've got to start on the mucking out."

"Can we help?" Zoe asked. She loved absolutely everything to do with animals –

ponies and donkeys especially!

"Well, I'm not sure," said Tim, looking over at Flo's dad.

"You're not really dressed for it, are you?" Flo's dad said. "You'll get all muddy!"

"Oh, please Dad!" Flo pleaded. "We've all got our trainers back in the car!"

The Glitter Girls had all changed into their wellies as soon as they had got out of the car, but they were all wearing their special Glitter Girl jackets that Hannah's mum had made them.

"We could take our jackets off, couldn't we?" Hannah said to the others.

"Course we could," said Charly, already removing hers. "I know it's September, but it's nice and warm out today!"

"Oh well, I suppose I could always go to the café and have a cup of coffee while you girls get on with it, if that's what you want."

"Go Glitter!" the girls replied.

Chapter 9

First thing on Monday morning, the Glitter Girls rushed in to see if Mrs Wadhurst knew how much money the Sponsored Silence had raised.

"I knew you wouldn't be able to wait," Mrs Wadhurst laughed. "But you're going to have to! Assembly in ten minutes – then you can find out! Now off you go to your classroom for registration!"

In the school hall, Mrs Wadhurst looked around at everyone.

"Well, boys and girls, if you can keep silent for me one more time I can tell you how much your quietness raised on Friday! We've done all our sums and worked out that we should have just over two hundred pounds towards the Donkey Sanctuary fund! Well done to all of you," Mrs Wadhurst looked around the room, smiling.

"Now don't forget the bring and buy sale and the cake sale this afternoon as soon as school's over. All the profits are going to the donkeys, so make sure you come along!"

The Glitter Girls looked at each other, smiling – almost laughing – with excitement.

"Go Glitter!" they whispered.

Everyone really had listened to what Mrs Wadhurst had said about the bring and buy sale because the tables in the school hall were piled high with goodies. Flo's dad had made some sweets and biscuits. Zoe's dad had given the Glitter Girls some seeds and plants that he had grown in his garden and they had been dis-played on a table with some plants that other parents had donated. Some of the boys and girls had brought in old board games and CDs that they didn't want any more and they were all on one table. Then, of course, there were the things that the Glitter Girls had made.

The Glitter Girls had been allowed to spend the last hour of school getting the hall ready and by half past three it was almost groaning with things to eat, wear, read and collect!

"Oh, I hope everyone buys something!" Zoe sighed.

"They will!" said Meg, determinedly as always.

"Looks like we're off!" said Hannah, as the first customers came hurrying through the door. Soon the hall was packed with people rummaging through piles of goodies.

The time sped by. The Glitter Girls were so busy selling things that they didn't have any more time for chatting.

"Phew!" said Hannah, as she sold the last of

the items on her table.

"Come on you lot," said Charly's mum. "Let's get everything cleared away and then we can count the money."

Charly, Hannah, Meg, Flo and Zoe got to work straight away and, with a little help from Mr Singh, the school caretaker, everything was soon put away so that the school hall was ready for the morning.

"Let's get counting then," said Meg, practical as ever. "You take that tin," she said, handing one biscuit tin full of money over to Zoe and Flo, "and we'll do this one."

★ ♥ ★ ♥ ★ ♥ ★

"We've got seventy-five pounds here," Flo said, a short while later.

"And we've got seventy pounds," Charly said.

"A hundred and forty-five pounds in total then," said Hannah. "That's not bad for an afternoon's work!"

"But it's not enough!" sighed Zoe.

"Come on, Zoe!" said Meg, sounding a bit angry. "We've already got the two hundred pounds from the Sponsored Silence, so this added to that takes us up to three hundred and forty-five pounds. We're doing our best!"

"But we need *five* hundred pounds!" Zoe shouted.

"And lots of other people are trying to raise money too! Like the football team, for a start!" Meg retorted.

The other Glitter Girls looked at Zoe and Meg in surprise. They hardly ever argued about anything!

"Come on, you two," said Zoe's mum. "Don't fall out. Zoe, I think you should apologize to Meg, don't you?"

Zoe's eyes were stinging with tears and she looked down at the floor. She felt really bad about shouting at her friend. She was just so desperate to save those donkeys!

"Friends?" Meg asked. She was feeling bad as well, for getting cross with Zoe.

"Yes, please!" said Zoe.

And the two Glitter Girls hugged.

"Go Glitter!" their three friends shouted in happiness!

By Tuesday morning, it seemed that everyone in school and almost everyone in town was wearing a SAVE THE DONKEYS badge! Word was fast getting around about the Glitter Girls efforts to raise enough money to secure the happiness of the two special donkeys at the Sanctuary. Even Zoe was looking a bit more cheerful!

At lunchtime, the girls went to see Mrs Wadhurst to tell her the good news about how much money had been raised at the bring and buy sale.

"Nearly there then, girls!" she said. "I'll ring the Donkey Sanctuary this afternoon and tell them how you are getting on. Now, how are things going with the disco?"

The Glitter Girls explained about how Jack was organizing all the music with one of his friends and Zoe's dad.

"And Mrs Bugden is doing all the food – bite-size pizzas and things like that," said Meg.

"And my mum's spoken to Mr Wix about the lighting and she's planning how to decorate the hall to make it look great," Hannah added.

"Excellent – I'm sure everyone has sorted their clothes for No Uniform Day," Mrs Wadhurst said. "I know I have! Well, it sounds like everything's going to plan then, doesn't it?"

"Go Glitter!" the girls replied.

★　♥　★　♥　★　♥　★

That afternoon, after school, the Glitter Girls met up in Hannah's bedroom. Charly was the last to arrive and, after collecting a plate of sandwiches from Hannah's mum in the kitchen, she climbed the stairs and knocked on the door of Hannah's room.

"Who's there?" Hannah asked.

"GG!" Charly replied.

She was a welcome sight to her friends who were starving after a busy day at school and eagerly began to tuck in.

"So, what have I missed?" asked Charly.

"Not much," Meg explained.

"No, we were just talking about the final arrangements for the disco," said Flo.

"My mum's sorted out the lighting – she borrowed some equipment from the theatre," Hannah explained.

"And Mr Wix is going to help set it up, along with the school music system," said Charly.

"Jack says he and his mate have everything ready," Meg added. "He's just desperate to be a DJ!"

"Great," said Zoe. "As long as he's going to be good!"

"Yes!" said Flo. "So, that's the really tricky stuff sorted. What else have we got to do?"

"We've got to speak to Mrs Bugden about the food," said Meg. "We'd better do that tomorrow – there are only a couple of days to go!"

"Is she just doing pizzas?" Charly asked.

"No – there's going to be salads and quiches as well. Little tiny ones that we can eat without knives and forks! And she's going to make a cake the shape of a donkey's head!"

"Wicked!" said Flo.

"How many tickets have we sold?" Hannah asked.

"Nearly all of them!" said Charly. "We've only got about twenty left to sell!"

"Well, let's see if we can sell them tomorrow," Meg decided.

"We can visit the shops in the High Street after school," Flo suggested.

"Good idea!" Zoe was looking pleased.

"Everyone's talking about what they're going

to wear for No Uniform Day as well," said Charly.

"I can't wait to see the teachers!"

"Nor me!" Flo grinned.

"Great! We've got two more events and a hundred and fifty-five pounds to go," Meg was checking things in her notebook.

"Do you think we'll make it?" Flo asked.

"We've got to!" Zoe said.

Chapter 10

It was Thursday afternoon and there was only one more day left to raise the money for the donkeys. After going home with Charly's mum and changing into some of their favourite clothes – including their special Glitter Girl jackets – Charly, Zoe, Meg, Flo and Hannah set off, determined to sell the last of the tickets for the disco. Within an hour, they had succeeded, and rushed back to Flo's house to work out how much money they had made from all of their ticket sales.

Over a packet of cookies, which they munched as they counted, the Glitter Girls added up fifty pounds.

"That makes a total of four hundred and five pounds!" said Meg.

"It isn't enough!" Zoe looked upset.

"All we need is another ninety-five pounds!" said Hannah.

"We've still got the disco to actually happen, haven't we?" said Charly.

"Yes," Flo added. "And we'll be selling the food that Mrs Bugden's doing as well as the drinks that Zoe's dad is organizing!"

"Oh yes," said Zoe, looking a bit brighter.

"And there's No Uniform Day tomorrow!" reminded Charly.

"We'll get there," said Meg. "We've got to save Pink and Fluffy!"

"Go Glitter!" they all cried.

On Friday morning, everyone came in wearing their own clothes. They loved the chance to wear jeans and trainers to school for a change. But when all the boys and girls saw their teachers, they couldn't stop laughing! All of the teachers were wearing school uniform. Even Mrs Wadhurst had a school tie on, to compliment her school sweatshirt and her lace-up shoes! Throughout the day, the teachers called all of the children "Sir" or "Miss", but no one dared to call Mrs Wadhurst by her first name. . . But then they didn't even know what it was!

Finally, it was Friday afternoon at last! With the help of Hannah's mum, who had brought all sorts of material and lights from the theatre where she worked, the Glitter Girls had transformed the school hall into a brilliant disco. They wondered if even Mrs Wadhurst would recognize it!

Charly, Zoe and Flo had decorated the walls with fantastic pictures of donkeys, just like the ones at the Sanctuary. Mr Wix arrived to help set up the lights and to get the music system going. Jack and his mate Billy arrived with boxes of CDs. They had dressed up in really cool Hawaiian shirts to get themselves into the party mood.

"It looks all right in here!" said Jack.

"Not bad!" agreed Billy.

Meg and Hannah were frantically laying out all the last plates of food with Mrs Bugden.

"Hey," Hannah's mum looked at the school clock. It was quarter past six and the disco was due to start at half past. "Hadn't you girls better get changed for the party?" she asked.

The Glitter Girls rushed off to the girls' changing rooms to get ready.

★ ♥ ★ ♥ ★ ♥ ★

Fifteen minutes later, the Glitter Girls were ready for action. They were all wearing their special Glitter Girl jackets, but they had different outfits on underneath. Flo was wearing a deep pink top with sparkles all over it and satin embroidered trousers. Zoe had an amazing outfit – she was dressed all in silver with a shiny skirt and matching boob tube. Charly was wearing a glittery skirt and backless top with multicoloured sequins sewn all over it that caught the light, and she had her favourite butterfly hair slides in her hair. Hannah's mum had made her a really great pair of trousers from black satin with diamanté detailing and Meg was wearing a soft velvet halterneck top – it was a gorgeous shade of pink and had a tiny heart embroidered on the side.

"Well, you look great!" said Charly's mum, who had arrived to help along with Zoe's dad. "And it looks like you've got some special visitors!" she added, nodding her head towards the door.

The Glitter Girls turned to look. It was Tim and the others from the Donkey Sanctuary. They had come like they said they would! And behind them the Glitter Girls could see lots of other children from school queuing to get in.

"Looks like the disco had better begin!" said Meg, and she rushed over to Jack and Billy and asked them if they could start the music.

★ ♥ ★ ♥ ★ ♥ ★

After half an hour, the Donkey Disco was packed. Zoe and Meg stood at the door, checking people's tickets, while Flo and Charly helped Mrs Bugden sell food and drink. Hannah ran around making sure that everyone was happy and taking drinks to her best friends.

"Well," said Meg, looking round the room and then at Zoe. "Looks like we could go and have a dance ourselves, now that everyone's here."

"Come on," said Zoe, smiling. "Let's boogie!"

"Tim's over there!" Meg pointed. "Let's go and join him!"

The girls rushed over, just in time to dance to the latest track from *S Club 7*.

"Hello," Meg said loudly over the music. "Thanks for coming today."

"We wouldn't have missed it," Tim said, smiling. "I've been hearing from your headteacher about all the hard work that you girls have been doing to raise money for the donkeys."

Christine from the Sanctuary was standing next to Tim. "How much have you got so far?" she asked.

"Four hundred and five pounds," said Zoe. "Still not enough. But we hope there will be more after the disco's finished tonight. We're so close! We've got to make some more. . ."

"Don't worry, Zoe, there should be a bit more from our No Uniform Day too," added Meg.

"You've done really well. The donkeys will really appreciate it. Hey," Tim said, pointing towards Mrs Wadhurst, who was waving at the Glitter Girls. "I think someone over there wants you."

Zoe and Meg turned to see the other Glitter Girls standing over by the food table with Mrs Wadhurst and another woman.

"See you later!" said Zoe, and she and Meg went to join the others.

The Glitter Girls recognized the lady with Mrs Wadhurst straight away. She was from the local paper and she'd talked to them back in the summer when the Glitter Girls had done the Magical Makeovers stall.

"Hello again, girls," she smiled.

"Hi!" they all said.

"I've just been hearing all about your efforts over the last two weeks. You know we've already been telling our readers about the two donkeys at the Sanctuary?" The Glitter Girls nodded. "Well, I understand that you are well on the way to raising the money to keep them there."

Excitedly, the girls explained about how much they had made.

"Well," the reporter said. "I've come to give you another contribution from the newspaper. We want to add a hundred pounds to your funds."

"Yeaaaaah!" the Glitter Girls shouted, almost drowning out the music.

"Do you think you could come to the Sanctuary tomorrow girls?" asked the reporter. "We'd like to take your photograph with the donkeys, if we can."

The Glitter Girls nodded – they wouldn't have missed it for the world!

"Go Glitter!" they all screamed!

★ ♥ ★ ♥ ★ ♥ ★

The next day, Zoe's mum took them along to the Donkey Sanctuary to meet up with the reporter and, more importantly, to see the two dear little donkeys again.

They were in their paddock, but they came over to greet the Glitter Girls straight away.

"I think they recognize our jackets!" Meg said, stroking the nose of one of them, while Zoe hugged the other.

"Hey, look at this," said Flo, pointing to a new sign that had been put up on the gate into the donkeys' paddock.

"What does it say?" Hannah asked.

Charly read it to them all: "We are delighted to inform you that donations towards keeping our new donkeys at the Sanctuary have raised one thousand and five pounds. We would especially like to thank the Glitter Girls who raised the largest amount of money for us, along with everyone else at Wells Road School."

"Wow!" sighed Zoe. Her dream had come true. The donkeys were safe.

Just then, Tim came over to see them.

"Hello again, girls!"

"Hello!" they all said.

"Good news, isn't it?" Tim said.

"Yes, but you forgot that we had some more money to count up after the disco!" Meg fished around in her pocket and brought out an envelope. "We got another fifty pounds from selling the food and the drink!"

"And thirty pounds from No Uniform Day!" said Charly.

"That is good news," Tim said. "And I've got something to tell you too!"

"What?" Hannah asked.

"We've chosen names for the donkeys as well!"

"What are they?" Zoe wondered aloud.

"Pink and Fluffy, just like you suggested," Tim smiled.

"Go Glitter!" the girls said, absolutely thrilled. "Pink and Fluffy!" they shouted. And as if they knew their names already, Pink and Fluffy joined in – braying loudly!

Don't miss:

Ballet Babes

Zoe looked out of her bedroom window and across her back garden. It was raining and it was cold. She would have begun to feel bored if she hadn't known that her best friends, Charly, Flo, Hannah and Meg, were going to arrive any minute. While she waited for them, Zoe looked around her bedroom. She'd decorated the walls with posters and pictures of horses, ponies and donkeys. Zoe loved animals and she wanted to be a vet when she was older.

Suddenly, there was a knock at the bedroom door.

RAT tat tat! It was the Glitter Girls' special knock!

"Who is it?" Zoe whispered.

"GG!" came the reply.

Immediately, Zoe opened her bedroom door. There stood Charly, Flo, Hannah and Meg. They were all smiling and ready to start the Glitter Girls' Sunday afternoon meeting!

★ ♥ ★ ♥ ★ ♥ ★

"Hi Zoe! I brought us these!" Meg said, walking in with a plate full of little cakes. Each of them was decorated with icing and covered with tiny sweets. They looked delicious!

"Hey, thanks!" Zoe said, taking the plate from her friend and putting it on her bedside table. "They look fab! Did you make them?"

"Yes – Sue helped me after lunch," explained

Meg. Sue was Meg's older sister.

"And I brought this up as well," said Charly, holding up a jug full of juice.

"Here are the cups," said Hannah, as she put down a collection of brightly coloured beakers next to the plate of cakes.

"I didn't bring anything with me . . . apart from this!" exclaimed Flo, taking off her bright pink mac and pulling a copy of the local paper out from underneath it. She shook off some rain, "Phew it's wet out there! So, have you lot seen this week's issue of the local paper?"

"No – why?" Meg asked, as she and the other Glitter Girls got comfy on the beanbags and cushions that were spread across Zoe's bedroom floor. Zoe had a great collection of them: some she'd made with the help of her older sisters. Others she'd either been given as presents or had saved up for and bought with her pocket money. Most of them were pink, but there were a few dark purple and mauve ones as well. And some had glittery thread shot through them and embroidery and jewels sewn into them. They were the perfect accessories for a Glitter Girl's bedroom!

"Well," said Flo dramatically, beginning to explain just why she'd brought the paper with her, "there's a story about the hospital radio in it."

"Really?" asked Charly, trying to grab the paper from Flo.

The Glitter Girls were always interested to hear more about the radio station. They'd once made a radio programme for the children in the hospital and occasionally they got asked back to help out.

"Come on Flo!" said Hannah, getting impatient. "Don't tease us! Tell us!"

"Yes, what does it say?" Zoe asked.

So Flo read the story to her friends:

" 'The hospital radio station is delighted to have taken delivery of a hundred new CDs. Thanks to the generosity of *Media TV viewers, Cindy Curtis, presenter of* Media Tonight, *donated a spectacular selection of the latest tracks to the hospital on their behalf.'* And there's a photo of Cindy giving the CDs to Suzy at the hospital."

"Cool!" said Charly, pushing her pink glasses back up her nose and grabbing the paper to look at it. "Isn't Cindy Curtis great?"

Each of the Glitter Girls looked at the story. They all had to agree with Charly. Cindy Curtis was really pretty and she always wore amazing clothes.

"We need another project like *Glitter FM*, don't we?" Meg asked her friends. "It was really good fun."

"Yes, wasn't it?" said Charly.

"Hey – cake anyone?" Zoe asked. She couldn't sit and look at Meg's delicious cakes any longer and handed them round to her friends.

Hannah was the last to look at the paper and,

once she'd finished reading about the hospital radio, she started to flick through the other pages, glancing at the pictures and the headlines. Suddenly, her eyes caught a big advertisement.

"Hey – listen to this, girls! There's going to be a big talent competition at the Town Hall!"

"Let's have a look!" said Zoe, leaning over Hannah's shoulder.

"Cool – I wonder who will enter?" Charly said.

A smile spread across Meg's face. "We could!" she said.

The other girls looked at her for a second, then they all began smiling and giggling.

"Go Glitter!" they all shouted.

When they had all calmed down a little bit, Meg, practical as ever, asked, "So when is this competition and how old do you have to be to enter?"

"Oh, don't say we won't be able to join in the fun!" said Charly anxiously.

"Let me look at the rules," said Hannah, who

still had the newspaper. She quickly read through the rules of entry that were printed next to the announcement for the competition.

"What does it say?" Zoe asked.

"Well," explained Hannah, "the competition is in four weeks' time and there are two sections to it. One's for people over sixteen and the other is for people below that age. That's us!"

Flo took her thumb out of her mouth. "Four weeks! That's not very long though, is it?"

"It would certainly be difficult for us to organize something for a talent competition in such a small amount of time," agreed Zoe.

"So, what are we going to do?" Charly asked. "Are we going to enter this competition or not?"